This book
belongs to

....

D0318528

Puddle's Fan Pages

Here's what other children have to say about their favourite puppy and his latest adventure!

"I liked the book a lot. I like the bit when Milo was bouncing on the tarpaulin. I liked it after Roxie charged at the tree. I think Roxie was the best character EVER! And my favourite person was Ruby." Piper, age 7

"I liked everything in the book, it was exciting and the best story ever. I really liked Milo the monkey." Samantha, age 6

"I like Puddle because he is cheeky and does things he's not supposed to do. He is clever because he helps out when things are missing or things go wrong. When he arrives he always brings an exciting adventure." Layla, age 7

"It was very exciting when they met Achak. I really like animals so I really liked this book. Puddle makes me laugh. Ruby and Harry are great, they are so adventurous." Ava, age 7

"This book is so funny. I love all the characters, but especially Puddle. I'm taking this book to school so my teacher can read it to my class and I'm going to ask my daddy if I can have a puppy ..." Poppy, age 6

Animal Antics

**Other books about
Puddle the Naughtiest Puppy:**

Puddle
the naughtiest puppy

Animal Antics

by Hayley Daze
illustrated by Ann Kronheimer
cover illustrated by Paul Hardman

A catalogue record for this book is available from the British Library

Published by Ladybird Books Ltd MMX
A Penguin Company
Penguin Books Ltd., 80 Strand, London WC2R 0RL, UK
Penguin Books Australia Ltd., Camberwell, Victoria, Australia
Penguin Group (NZ) 67 Apollo Drive, Rosedale,
North Shore 0632, New Zealand

1 3 5 7 9 10 8 6 4 2
Series created by Working Partners Limited, London W6 0QT
Text © Working Partners Ltd MMX
Cover illustration © Working Partners Ltd MMX
Interior illustrations © Ladybird Books Ltd MMX

Special thanks to Jane Clarke

ISBN: 978-1-40930-403-6
Printed in England

Mixed Sources

Product group from well-managed
forests and other controlled sources
www.fsc.org   Cert no. SA-COC-001592
© 1996 Forest Stewardship Council

FSC

*To Margaret and Robin, with many thanks
for all the brilliant Butler B&Bs!*

When clouds fill the sky and rain starts to fall,
Ruby and Harry are not sad at all.
They know that when puddles appear on the ground,
A magical puppy will soon be around!

Puddle's his name, and he's the one
Who can lead you to worlds of adventure and fun!
He may be quite naughty, but he's clever too,
So come follow Puddle – he's waiting for you!

A present from Puddle:

Look out for the special code at the back of the book to
get extra-special games and loads of free stuff at Puddle's
website! Come and play at www.puddlethepuppy.com

Contents

Chapter One
The Case of the Disappearing Puppy

"Aha!" cried Ruby, picking up the magnifying glass on Grandad's desk. "Now Chief Inspector Ruby, the great Animal Detective, can search for clues to solve the Mystery of the Missing Platypus!"

Her cousin Harry looked at her over the top of his glasses.

"You don't need a magnifying

glass to find your toy duck-billed platypus," he told Ruby. "You just need to remember where you left it."

Harry turned over the cushion on Grandad's chair. "Nothing under here," he said.

"I remember bringing him into Grandad's study when I was looking for a book to read . . ." Ruby held the magnifying glass to her eye and scanned the books in Grandad's

bookcase. She could see her fingerprints in a thin layer of dust where she'd taken out a book, but there was no sign of Teddy, her toy duck-billed platypus.

"Perhaps I put Teddy down somewhere," she murmured.

Ruby's plaits swung as she dropped to her knees to search under the desk. Her tummy did a somersault. There was a faint line of muddy paw prints

17

on the study floor. Puppy paw prints!

"Harry, look!" she cried. "Puddle's been here!"

"Let me see." Harry took the magnifying glass and knelt down to examine the prints.

"They're still damp!" he exclaimed. A big smile spread across his face. "It must be raining again."

Ruby clapped her hands in delight.

Whenever it rained, the little puppy arrived and they went on amazing adventures together.

"Where did Puddle go?" she wondered aloud. "He's disappeared, like Teddy."

"Let's hunt for Teddy later," Harry said. "Right now, we have to crack the Case of the Disappearing Puppy!" He pushed his glasses up his nose. "I've been reading a book called *Whodunnit*," he said. "It's all about how detectives solve mysteries. These paw prints are clues. We can track them."

Harry set off across the study floor on his hands and knees, holding the

magnifying glass above the faint
prints.

Ruby was close behind Harry
as they followed the trail under
Grandad's chair, out of the study,
along the hallway and into the
kitchen. The back door of the cottage

was ajar and the muddy prints led outside.

Ruby and Harry jumped to their feet and pulled on their wellies.

"Quick!" Harry said. "We have to follow Puddle's prints before the rain washes them away."

"They're heading for Grandad's vegetable patch," Ruby said as they dashed up the garden path. The rain was falling harder now and the paw prints were already fading.

"Puddle, where are you?" Ruby called.

Nearby, one of Grandad's lettuces started to shake. Ruby stared at it. A little white muzzle with a black rubbery nose was poking out from the middle. The lettuce leaves surrounded it like a bright green mane.

"Puddle!" Ruby laughed. "You look just like a little green lion."

"Woof!" Puddle barked. He leapt

out of the lettuce, sending leaves flying everywhere, and licked Ruby's nose.

"Yuck!" Ruby spluttered.

"There goes one of Grandad's prize-winning lettuces," Harry groaned.

Puddle ran up to a big puddle that had formed in a dip in the path. He slowly circled it, then turned back to

Ruby and Harry, wagging his tail.

"Woof! Woof!" he barked.
"WOOF!" And he leapt into the
puddle and disappeared in a shower
of raindrops!

Ruby glanced at Harry and tugged
on her plaits for luck.

"Adventure time!" she squealed
as they jumped in after the naughty
little puppy.

Chapter Two
Going Wild

Ruby opened her eyes. She, Harry
and Puddle were standing in the
middle of a grassy landscape. But the
grass wasn't short, green and damp
– it was tall, dry and yellow, like
straw. And the sky above them wasn't
grey and cloudy – it was a clear and
brilliant blue.

"Phew, it's hot," Harry muttered.

"My glasses are steaming up." He took them off and polished them on his sleeve.

Ruby shaded her eyes from the hot sun and looked around. In the distance, she could make out a tall tree and a group of huts shimmering under a haze of heat. Close to where they were standing, a puff of sandy-brown smoke was getting bigger and bigger.

Ruby pointed it out to Harry. "Is that a fire?" she asked.

Harry put his glasses back on. "I don't think so," he murmured. "I can't see any flames. It must be a dust storm."

"But there's no wind," Ruby muttered.

A snort came out of the cloud of dust. A cold shiver ran down Ruby's spine. In the middle of the cloud, she could see a shadowy shape, with a broad stocky body and a horn on the end of its nose. It was pawing at the ground with its sturdy front legs.

"Yip, yip, yip!" Puddle yapped in alarm.

"It's a baby rhinoceros,"
Harry whispered. "I've seen TV
programmes about rhinos. They paw
at the ground like that when they're
about to charge."

"Charge?" Ruby gulped. "If it
charges, it will flatten us!"

Harry turned to Ruby. "Run!"
he yelled.

Ruby, Harry and Puddle crashed through the long yellow grass. Ruby could feel her heart pounding. She glanced down at Puddle. His tongue was hanging out as he panted for breath.

"Watch out!" Ruby shouted, dodging out of the way of an ostrich.

The huge bird strode past them in a flurry of feathers.

They burst out of the high grass and skidded to a halt. Right in front of them was a waterhole. A big grey head broke the surface of the water and yawned, showing its enormous teeth. One of its bottom teeth was missing.

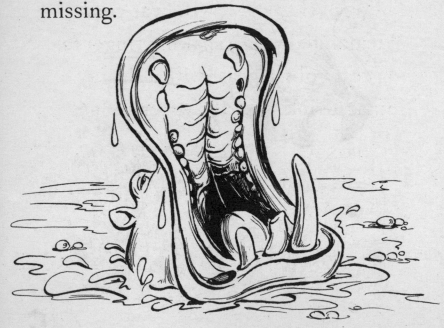

"That was a hippo!" Harry exclaimed, as the head sank back beneath the water. "It needs to see a dentist."

"If I was an animal dentist," Ruby whispered, "I'd make it a false tooth and . . ."

"*Shhh!*" Harry hissed. "There's a lion over there! It will hear you." He pointed with a shaking finger to a great golden beast with a shaggy mane, drinking at the water's edge.

Puddle whimpered and hid behind Ruby's wellies. Ruby could feel him shaking from nose to tail.

"Which way do we run?" Harry whispered in a trembly voice. "There's a lion in front of us and a rhino behind us."

As he spoke, the lion opened its mouth, displaying its razor-sharp fangs.

Puddle lay down and put his paws over his eyes.

Ruby was so scared that her feet wouldn't budge. She was rooted to the spot! She glanced at Harry. Behind his glasses, his eyes were squeezed tight shut. He was frozen with fear. Ruby closed her eyes, too.

"Please don't gobble us up!" she whispered.

Chapter Three
The Safari Rescue Park

Eeep! Eeep!

A strange high-pitched squeaking filled the air, followed by a rumble that sounded a lot like purring. Ruby slowly opened her eyes. The noises were coming from the lion!

It was gazing happily at a boy who had emerged out of the long grass. The boy had binoculars slung around his neck, and a pink blanket draped over one arm.

Ruby nudged Harry and Puddle. Harry opened his eyes. His mouth fell open.

"Don't worry about Leo," the boy called out. "He wouldn't hurt a fly. He's an old softie."

"You must be a lion tamer," Ruby sighed with relief. "We're very, very pleased to see you. My name's Ruby, and this is my cousin Harry, and Puddle the puppy."

Puddle wagged his tail, but stayed behind Ruby.

"I'm Achak," the boy told them with a grin. "I'm not a lion tamer. I just work here."

Harry peered at him over the top of his glasses. "What exactly is 'here'?" he asked.

"Safari Rescue Park," Achak said. "We take in animals who have been mistreated, or orphaned, or have something wrong with them, and we look after them and make them better. Our goal is to get all our animals back to the wild."

"That's a brilliant thing to do,"

39

Ruby said, and smiled.

"It must be a great job," Harry said.

"It is when everything goes well," Achak agreed. "But I don't think we'll ever manage to get Leo back to the wild." Achak pointed to the lion as it padded off into the grass. "Leo seems to have forgotten how to roar. But he likes living here."

"What about the little rhino?"

Harry asked. "We thought it was going to charge at us."

"Roxie?" Achak laughed. "Roxie's never learned how to charge. She was orphaned when she was a tiny baby."

"But she was pawing at the ground," Ruby told him.

"She's probably upset because she's lost her comfort blanket," Achak explained, taking the pink blanket off his arm to show them. "We wrapped her in this when she first came to us, and now she takes it everywhere. I'm

on my way to find her to give it back."

"A rhino with a comfort blanket." Ruby giggled. "Only little children have those."

Harry pushed his glasses up his nose. "I still have mine," he declared. "I can't sleep without it." He took the pink blanket from Achak and held it up. "But my blanket isn't pink, and it doesn't smell of baby rhino," he said, holding his nose.

"It's full of holes!" Ruby exclaimed. "You must have big moths here."

"That was Roxie." Achak laughed. "She likes to stick her horn into it."

Puddle poked his nose out from behind Ruby's wellies and stared at the blanket. He sniffed deeply.

"*Atchoo!*" he sneezed.

"I don't think he likes the smell of rhino," Ruby said, watching Puddle's ears go back.

"Grrr!" Puddle growled. Then he dashed out from behind Ruby's legs and charged towards the blanket. Harry swished it out of the naughty little puppy's way.

"Harry, you look like a matador

waving his cloak at a tiny little
bull," Ruby said, giggling as Puddle
jumped up and down, trying to grab
the blanket.

"I've read about matadors..."
Harry said, handing the blanket back
to Achak. He scratched his head.
"Matadors wave their red cloaks at
bulls so the bulls will charge at them.

So maybe we can wave a pink blanket at a rhino . . ."

". . . and teach Roxie how to charge!" Ruby clapped her hands. "That's a brilliant idea, Harry! Let's see if it works."

"We have to find her, first," Achak said with a smile.

"No problem," Harry told him. "We trampled down the grass when we ran away from her, so it will be easy to follow our tracks back to Roxie."

Ruby, Harry, Puddle and Achak followed the trail they had made through the tall grass. As they approached the clearing, a gentle snoring noise filled the warm air. Roxie was having a nap.

"Wooooof!" Puddle barked at the little rhino.

Roxie struggled to her feet and stared sleepily at them.

Ruby and Harry took Roxie's pink comfort blanket from Achak and stepped towards her, each holding a corner of the blanket.

"Come on, Roxie!" they shouted.

Roxie's eyes opened wide. She gave a great snort.

Ruby and Harry flapped the pink blanket so it billowed and waved in the bright sunshine.

"Charge!" they yelled.

Roxie churned up the dusty earth with her feet.

"She doesn't know what to do," Harry murmured.

Puddle ran up to Roxie. "Woof!" he barked, then he turned and raced towards the blanket.

Roxie tipped her horned head and thundered after Puddle. Puddle dodged under the blanket.

"Yes!" Achak, Ruby and Harry

shouted in triumph as Roxie charged off with the blanket stuck on her horn.

"Yip, yip!" Puddle yapped, racing after her.

"Isn't it great?" Ruby said to Harry.

"Now Roxie's learned how to charge, she can go back to the wild."

"But Puddle's going with her," Harry retorted, as they watched Puddle and Roxie disappear into the heat haze. "And we need Puddle to get back to Grandad's."

Ruby stared at Harry.

"If Puddle follows Roxie into the wild," she cried, "we'll never find our way home!"

Chapter Four
Feeding Time

"Roxie's running back to the Safari Rescue Park," Achak laughed. "Puddle will follow her there. It's feeding time. Would you like to help?"

"Yes please!" Ruby and Harry said together.

Achak led the way to a group of wooden buildings with straw roofs.

The wood was painted yellow so that
the buildings seemed to be part of the
grassy plain.

The little rhino and the old lion
were waiting in the shade outside
the largest hut, with Puddle sitting
beside them wagging his tail. They
got to their feet when they saw Achak.

"This is where we keep the food,"
Achak told Ruby, Harry and Puddle
as he unlatched the door to let them in.

There were barrels and boxes everywhere, covered with dark green oilskin blankets. Ruby lifted one of the heavy tarpaulins and peered into a barrel. It was full of brightly coloured fruit.

Achak handed Ruby and Harry a bucket each.

"I'll feed Leo," Achak said. "Harry, fill your bucket with bananas for Milo, please."

"Who is Milo?" Harry asked, lifting the tarpaulin on the fruit barrel.

"A very cheeky monkey," Achak said. "It's strange that he's not here. I'll call him." Achak cupped his hands around his mouth. "Milo! Dinner time!"

Harry glanced up from the fruit barrel. "I can see oranges, mangoes, papayas and pineapples," he said. "But I can't see any bananas."

"There was definitely a bunch of bananas in there yesterday," Achak said. "That cheeky Milo must have unlatched the door and taken them."

"That is naughty," Harry said.

"Even Puddle can't do that."

"Milo will do anything for bananas," Achak said with a grin, "except climb a banana tree. He's scared of heights."

"That's a big problem for a monkey," Ruby said. "They live in trees."

"Milo doesn't live in a tree – he lives in a den behind the hut," Achak said. "Maybe he took the bananas back there..."

"I'll check," Harry said, rushing off.

Ruby half expected Puddle to run after Harry, but the little puppy was busy sniffing round every container of food.

"I'll find you some food later, Puddle," Ruby told him. "What does Roxie eat, Achak?"

"She has special food with extra vitamins to help her grow. It's in that box over there." Achak pointed to a large wooden crate labelled *Rhino Pellets*.

Ruby heaved the heavy tarpaulin off the crate. It was full of what looked like crunchy, munchy, shredded-wheat biscuits.

"Yip!" Puddle barked, and before Ruby could stop him, he hurled himself into the crate and began to gobble up the pellets. Ruby could just see his tail sticking out.

"Here, Puddle. Have some of Henrietta the hyena's food," Achak said, scattering a handful of small bone-shaped biscuits on the ground.

Puddle's tail wagged as he crunched them up.

Achak took a lump of meat out of a
cool box and threw it outside to Leo.
Ruby took the bucket of rhino pellets
and put it down in front of Roxie.
The little rhino buried her nose in the
bucket. Ruby patted Roxie's leathery
head as she chomped up her food.
She still had her comfort blanket
wrapped around her horn.

Harry appeared at Achak and Ruby's side. "Milo's not in his den," he panted.

"I wonder where he is." Achak lifted his binoculars to his eyes and scanned the grassland. "I can't see any sign of him," he said. "Can you?" He handed the binoculars to Harry.

Harry held the binoculars in front of his glasses. He fiddled with the dial on the central hinge. "I can't see any monkeys either," he declared.

"Let me see!" Ruby took the binoculars and put them to her eyes. "Everything's blurred," she said, with a sigh of disappointment.

"You have to focus them for your

eyes," Harry told her.

Ruby was puzzled.

"Turn this until you can see clearly," Harry explained, pointing out the dial.

Ruby twisted it from side to side.

"Wow!" she said, as the grassland popped into focus. In the foreground she could see the individual blades of grass. "These binoculars are brilliant. They're even better than Grandad's magnifying glass!"

Ruby took the binoculars away from her eyes and turned them round so she was looking through the large lenses at the other end.

"This way everything is tiny," she

laughed, kneeling down and focusing the binoculars on Puddle. "You're a mouse-sized puppy now."

Puddle ran up and peered curiously at the binoculars. Ruby held them steadily at arm's length so he could see through them.

"Woof!" Puddle barked in surprise. Then, "Grrr!" he growled,

as he stared through the binoculars at Ruby. "Grrr! Grrr!"

"It's OK, Puddle," Ruby laughed, handing the binoculars back to Achak. "I haven't turned into a giant."

Puddle looked at her and wagged his tail.

"Maybe I will be able to see Milo from up here." Achak scrambled up on to the roof of the feeding hut and focused his binoculars towards the waterhole. "There's no sign of him," he said, in alarm. "Milo's disappeared!"

Chapter Five
Monkey Business

"Don't worry!" Ruby called up reassuringly. "Harry, Puddle and I will help you find Milo. We're animal detectives!"

"First we should check for clues in Milo's den," Harry said, leading the way to Milo's hut. It smelled of fresh straw.

"I gave him new bedding this

morning," Achak told them.

Ruby looked at the undisturbed straw. "It doesn't look as if Milo has been here," she said.

"He loves playing with people," Achak said, leading them round the back of Milo's den. "If we play on his monkey playground, maybe he'll hear us and come and join in."

"That's a brilliant idea!" Ruby exclaimed. She raced up the steps of a long steep slide, closely followed by Harry.

"Wheeeee!" they squealed as they

slid down it on their bottoms.

"I've never seen Milo go on the slide," Achak said, "I think it's too high for him. Try the swings. He likes those."

Ruby and Harry clambered into two old tyres that were hanging from a wooden frame. Achak gave them a shove.

"Whoooaaaaa!" they roared as they soared through the air.

"Yip!" Puddle yapped. "Yip, yip!"

"It's no good," Achak sighed. "Milo isn't coming."

Ruby and Harry clambered out of the swings. Puddle raced up to them. He had something in his mouth.

"You can't still be hungry, Puddle," Ruby groaned.

Puddle dropped the object he was carrying at Ruby and Harry's feet. It was a mottled brown-yellow colour, and it was floppy and slimy.

"It's a banana skin!" Harry said. "Well done, Puddle. You're using your detective skills."

"It's a clue!" Ruby said. "Are there any more?"

Puddle and the children searched through the woodchips on the floor of the monkey playground.

"Here's another one," cried Ruby, bending under the slide.

"And another!" Harry said, pointing to the edge of the grassland.

"And here's a trail of trampled grass. We can follow it!"

Ruby, Harry, Achak and Puddle set out along the trail. Puddle kept his nose to the ground, and every so often he snuffled out a banana skin.

"This is definitely Milo's trail," Ruby declared. "He must have eaten that whole bunch of bananas."

"Then he's probably gone off looking for more," Achak said.

Sure enough, the trail led to the foot of a tall banana tree. Puddle raised his nose into the air and sniffed deeply.

"Wooooooof!" he barked.

Ruby looked up into the broad

green leaves. At the top of the tree, a thick stalk was growing from the centre of the stem. The biggest bunch of bananas that Ruby had ever seen was dangling from it. And a little monkey was clinging to the bunch of bananas!

"Milo!" Ruby exclaimed. The monkey turned his head and stared down at her.

"*Oop!*" Milo hooted. "*Ooop! Oooop!*"

"Come down, Milo!" Achak called. But Milo didn't budge.

Ruby took the binoculars. Milo's arms, legs and tail were all tightly wrapped round the bananas, and he was quivering from nose to tail. His eyes were wide with fear.

"He's stuck!" Ruby said, handing the binoculars to Harry. "What's he doing up there if he's scared of heights?"

Harry examined the tree through the binoculars. "Detectives have to piece together the evidence," he said. "The bananas are very ripe. And we know Milo had finished the bunch he took from the food hut. So he must have smelled these bananas, and not been able to resist them..."

"And he climbed up, but then he got too frightened to climb down," Achak added. He grinned. "I can be a detective, too! Now, how do we get him down?"

"I'm good at climbing," Ruby said. "I'll climb up and show Milo how to climb back down." She looked at the branchless trunk of the banana tree. "I'll need a boost up," she told Harry and Achak.

Harry and Achak laced their fingers together. Ruby put her foot in their cupped hands and stepped up, trying to grip the tree, but it was no good. The thick trunk of the banana tree was much too slippery for her to climb.

There was a sudden loud *creeeaaak!*

Milo, and the bunch of ripe bananas he was clinging to, swayed wildly in the air.

"*OOOOOOP!*" Milo hooted in alarm. A couple of bananas fell and splattered on the hard earth beneath the tree. Puddle jumped back with a startled, "Yip!"

Ruby took the binoculars and focused them on the top of the tree.

"Oh no!" she groaned. "That whole stalk of bananas is about to break off. We have to get Milo down, fast!"

Chapter Six
The Puppy Trampoline

Harry frowned as he watched Puddle sniff at the gooey remains of the splattered bananas. "Milo will be badly hurt if he falls," he said.

"If only we had something bouncy for Milo to land on," Ruby said. "Like a trampoline . . ."

"Or a blanket like firefighters hold when someone jumps out of a blazing building," Harry agreed. "Roxie's got a blanket, but it isn't strong enough – it's full of holes."

"The tarpaulins that cover the animal feed are strong enough!" Ruby exclaimed.

"I'll fetch one!" Achak took to his heels and raced back to the huts.

Ruby, Harry and Puddle gazed nervously at the banana tree. Another banana splattered at their feet, and another and another. At last Achak

reappeared, panting and dragging the heavy tarpaulin after him.

They held it out beneath the terrified monkey.

"Jump, Milo!" they called. "Jump!"

But Milo didn't move.

"He doesn't understand that he should jump on to the tarpaulin," Achak groaned.

"We'll have to show him," Ruby said. "Put the tarpaulin on the ground for a moment."

Harry and Achak looked puzzled as they lowered it.

"Come on, Puddle!" Ruby patted the middle of the tarpaulin. The little puppy bounded on to it.

"Pull it tight," Ruby ordered Harry and Achak. The three of them dug their heels into the ground and tugged at the tarpaulin.

Boing! Puddle bounced into the air

as the tarpaulin went taut. He landed
back in the middle of it.

"Yip, yip, yip!" he yapped happily
as he *boing-boing-boinged* on the
tarpaulin.

"Look, Milo, it's fun. It's a
trampoline!" Ruby giggled.

The little monkey glanced down
and tightened his grip on the bananas.

Puddle sprang off the tarpaulin,
wagging his tail.

There was another loud *creeeaaak!*

"At this rate we'll have to catch
Milo and the bananas in the
tarpaulin," Achak said.

"How do we get Milo to let go of the bananas?" Harry asked, scratching his head.

"I know!" Ruby's face lit up. She dropped the corner of the tarpaulin she was holding. "You stay here," she told the boys. "I know who can help!"

Puddle ran after her as she rushed off through the grass.

Chapter Seven
Roxie Charges In

Roxie the little rhinoceros still had her nose in the bucket of food and her comfort blanket wrapped round her horn when Ruby dashed up to her, panting.

"Come on, Roxie!" Ruby grabbed a handful of crunchy rhino pellets and set off down the trail. Roxie took her nose out of the bucket and stared at her.

"This way, Roxie!" Ruby flattened her palm and held the pellets under Roxie's nose, but the little rhino didn't move.

Ruby ran round behind her, leaned against Roxie's leathery bottom and shoved. But the little rhino still

wouldn't budge. Ruby's heart sank.

"We're running out of time," she groaned, just as Puddle raced up, barking. Roxie glared at the little puppy. She lowered her horn towards him. The pink comfort blanket flopped over her eyes.

"Grrr!" Puddle growled. He

dashed up and grabbed Roxie's
blanket between his teeth and raced
down the track towards the banana
tree. The pink blanket fluttered
behind him as he ran.

"Give it back to Roxie, you naughty
little puppy!" Ruby gasped, dropping
the pellets as she dashed after him.
Behind them, there was a

tremendous snort. Ruby glanced
back over her shoulder. A cloud of
dust was rising above the grass. The
ground began to tremble. Ruby's
heart leapt. Roxie was charging after
her blanket!

Puddle and Ruby skidded to a halt in front of the banana tree.

"Get the tarpaulin ready!" Ruby shouted to Harry and Achak.

She grabbed Roxie's blanket from Puddle's jaws and draped it round the tree trunk.

"Roxie will charge the tree and shake Milo down," she explained to the boys, grabbing an edge of the tarpaulin just as Roxie thundered into view. Ruby gasped in surprise. Leo was racing after the little rhinoceros!

Roxie and Leo screeched to a halt in front of the banana tree. Roxie's beady little eyes were fixed on the pink comfort blanket sticking to the tree trunk.

"Charge, Roxie, charge!" Ruby, Harry and Achak shouted.

"Hooray!" they cheered as Roxie lowered her head and thundered towards her blanket.

Thwack!

The trunk of the banana tree shook when Roxie bulldozed into it. High above, the leaves rustled – and with a startled, "*Oooooooop!*" Milo let go of the bunch of bananas and landed in the tarpaulin.

Kerplunk!

Milo jumped into Achak's arms and wrapped his legs and tail round him, all the while hooting with joy.

Above them, the tree gave a humongous *creee . . . ak . . . ak*.

Ruby, Harry, Achak and Milo jumped out of the way as the heavy bunch of bananas crashed to the ground, narrowly missing Leo.

"Roooooooooaaaaaaaaar!" the lion roared in surprise.

Puddle jumped into Ruby's arms.

Chapter Eight
Bouncing Back

"*Rooooaaar!*" Leo roared as he trotted off into the grassland.

"Leo's learned how to roar." Ruby laughed as she set Puddle down on the tarpaulin.

"Woof!" Puddle barked, jumping up and down. "Woof! Woof!"

"He wants another go on the trampoline!" Harry said.

Harry, Ruby and Achak picked up the tarpaulin and held it taut.

Puddle barked in delight as he soared into the air. Milo watched as the little puppy bounced higher and higher and higher.

"Milo wants to join in the fun," Achak said as the monkey leapt on to the trampoline and did a little bounce.

"OOOP!" Milo hooted, waving his arms in the air. Soon he was bouncing as high as Puddle. The cheeky little monkey somersaulted right over the top of the puppy!

"Puddle's made Leo roar and helped Milo to get over his fear of heights," Achak chuckled. "But my arms are getting tired."

Ruby, Harry and Achak lowered
the tarpaulin to the ground. Milo
jumped into Achak's arms again.
Ruby giggled as the cheeky monkey
pursed his lips and blew kisses at
them all.

"Yip, yip, yip!" Puddle yapped,
and he began to run round and round
Ruby and Harry. Everything started
to go hazy.

"We have to go now," Ruby told

Achak. "Say goodbye to all the animals for us."

"I will! Thanks for your help," Achak called. "I couldn't have done it without you!"

The Safari Rescue Park blurred, and in no time at all, Ruby, Harry and Puddle were standing next to Grandad's vegetable patch once more. The sun was shining brightly and the big puddle that had transported them to the Safari Rescue Park was now just a damp stain.

"Woof!" Puddle barked and then, with a wag of his tail, he disappeared into the lettuces.

Ruby reached for him but, instead of a furry little puppy, she found her toy duck-billed platypus.

"Teddy!" she exclaimed, picking up her toy and giving him a hug. There was a pair of binoculars dangling from his beak that looked just like Achak's! Ruby handed them to Harry.

"These are perfect for looking for things," Harry said as he put them around his neck.

"The Mystery of the Missing Platypus is solved!" Ruby grinned, giving Harry a high-five. "And it's all thanks to Puddle and another magical rainy day!"

Can't wait to find out
what Puddle will do next?
Then read on! Here is
the first chapter from
Puddle's ninth adventure,
Christmas Snow Puppy . . .

Christmas
Snow Puppy

Snow squished between the fingers of Ruby's red gloves as she rolled the snowball in her hands, getting ready to take aim at her cousin Harry.

"That's not how to make a snowman," Harry said, pushing his glasses back into place with his snowy mitten. "You roll the snowball on the ground to make it bigger, like this."

"Then can I throw it?" Ruby giggled. Harry rolled his eyes and smiled at Ruby. "Just kidding," she said.

Ruby looked back at Grandad's cottage. It was just like the front of a Christmas card, all dusted with snow.

Inside, everyone was crammed into Grandad's kitchen. Mum was making her special parsnip, peach and pistachio stuffing and Uncle Dan, Harry's dad, was busy measuring ingredients for his trifle.

Ruby and Harry had been told to play outside as they were "getting under everyone's feet", which didn't make sense at all to Ruby. *Nobody stepped on us!* she thought.

Ruby was glad their families were spending the winter holiday together, but she wished there was more snow. They had used up most of the snow on the grass already, and their snowman still only came up to Ruby's knees.

"I'm just making the head into a perfect sphere," Harry said.

"I don't want a head like a spear," Ruby said.

"No, a sphere." Harry paused. "Like a football shape." He rolled it over and they lifted the snowball on to the body. Both cousins stood back and looked at their creation.

"It doesn't look much like a snowman . . . " Harry started.

"More like a snow puppy," Ruby said with a smile. "Now for some finishing touches."

Ruby looked at the odds and ends they had dragged out of Grandad's hall cupboard.

Harry found two big black buttons to use for eyes. Then they picked up Grandad's slippers and put one on each side of the head for the puppy's ears.

"It's starting to look like someone we know," Harry said.

Ruby smiled as she remembered all

the magical adventures they had been on with Puddle, a naughty puppy who arrived whenever it rained.

Fluffy flakes of snow started fluttering to the ground around them. *I wonder if Puddle will come to see us when it snows, too,* she thought.

Almost as if he'd read her mind, the real Puddle scampered out from the hedge and bounded across the garden towards Ruby and Harry, slipping and sliding on the slushy snow.

"Puddle!" they shouted. "Watch out for the . . ."

Puddle crashed into the snow puppy, sending buttons and slippers flying across the garden.

"Puddle, you naughty puppy,"
Harry said, wiping the snow from his
glasses.

Ruby squealed. "Now we can have a
snowy adventure!"

"Woof, woof," Puddle barked as
if in agreement. He shook himself
from nose to tail and raced along
the garden path. He sniffed at the
icy puddles. Then the puppy took
a running jump at one of the bigger
pools.

Splat!

Instead of jumping through it,
Puddle slid across the ice on his
tummy, spread out like a starfish.

"Oh no," Harry said. "He can't

jump through the puddle if it's frozen!"

Ruby sighed. "Maybe we can't have our winter adventure after all."

**

To find out what happens next,
get your copy of
CHRISTMAS SNOW PUPPY!
Coming soon ...

Puddle
the naughtiest puppy

Magic Mayhem

Ruby and Harry are amazed to find themselves in a medieval castle . . .

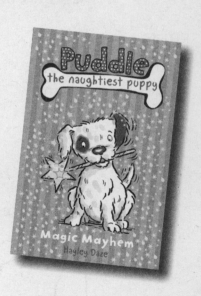

. . . when Puddle takes them on their latest adventure! They meet a magician's apprentice who is in deep trouble. He's lost his spell book. Can Puddle save the day?

Find out in MAGIC MAYHEM . . .

Pirate Surprise

Can you imagine what it's like to sail on a pirate ship?

Ruby and Harry find out – when Puddle takes them on an amazing adventure on the high seas! Captain Redbeard has a bad case of the hiccups! Will Puddle be able to cure him?

Find out in PIRATE SURPRISE...

Christmas Snow Puppy

Go on a festive adventure with Ruby, Harry and Puddle!

The children find themselves in a beautiful winter wonderland. Can they get through the snow to the big winter festival on time?

Find out in CHRISTMAS SNOW PUPPY...
Coming soon!

Star of the School

Join Puddle, Ruby and Harry on their new adventure in the Wild West!

Lil the littlest cowgirl is told she is too small to join the cowboy school. But with Puddle's help, can she prove herself by catching Outlaw Pete?

Find out in STAR OF THE SCHOOL...

Holiday Musical

Go on an amazing Hollywood adventure
with Ruby, Harry and Puddle!

The children are
thrilled when they
get to star in a new
movie. But the
director thinks
Puddle has stolen
the script! How can
Puddle show he's
not to blame?

Find out in HOLIDAY MUSICAL…

Going to the Vet

Hi, it's Ruby and Harry again with Puddle! That was a brilliant adventure, wasn't it? Now, let's find out a few more things about real dogs!

This time, Dogs Trust are going to teach us about how important it is to take your dog to the vet.

Dogs can sometimes get ill, just like you or me. So if your dog is feeling unwell, don't worry, you and your parents just need to take him to the vet. There, they will soon find out what is wrong with your four-legged friend and will help make him better by giving him some medicine. The vet will probably also tell you to let your dog relax and recover.

Always remember, Puddle is a magical dog, while real dogs and puppies are living animals who need a lot of care, love and attention.

Dog Health

• Never forget that all dogs need regular check-ups — just like us humans — to make sure that they are healthy and happy!

• Can you think of a time when you have had to go to the doctor because you were ill? Or maybe visit your dentist for a check-up?

• Now you know about how important it is to take your dog to the vet, why not talk about it with your friends — maybe they can share with you what they know about taking their pet to the vet!

Next time, join us for our Christmas Special! We can't wait! See you then.

Safari Scramble!

Look at the strange words below.
Can you unscramble each one to make
the name of an animal from the story?
Then match each word to a picture.

1. **exior**
2. **oel**
3. **delpud**
4. **liom**

A

B

C

D

Spot the Difference!

Study the picture of Ruby, Harry and Achak below and then look at the one on the opposite page. Can you spot six tricky differences?

Answers on the next page

Answers to Puddle Puzzles:

Safari Scramble: 1. Roxie - C; 2. Leo - B; 3. Puddle - D; 4. Milo - A

Spot the Difference: The hut roof has changed, Achak's T-shirt is black, Harry's hair has changed, Ruby's plait has gone, one of the buckets has gone, part of the tree has gone

For more magical adventures, come and play with Puddle at

www.puddlethepuppy.com

Use this special code to get extra special games and free stuff at puddlethepuppy.com

BINOCULARS